Renew by phone or online
0845 0020 777
www.bristol.gov.uk/libraries
Bristol Libraries

PLEASE RETURN BOOK BY LAST DATE STAMPED

BR100

21055 Print Services

ORCHARD BOOKS

Visit Michael Coleman's website!
www.michael-coleman.com

More Angels FC books to look out for...

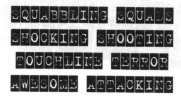

SQUABBLING SQUADS
SHOCKING SHOOTING
TOUCHLINE TERROR
AWESOME ATTACKING

ORCHARD BOOKS
338 Euston Road,
London NW1 3BH
Orchard Books Australia
Hachette Children's Books
Level 17/207 Kent Street, Sydney, NSW 2000
First published in Great Britain as individual volumes
First published in Great Britain in this format 2004
Dazzling Dribbling
Text © Michael Coleman 1999, inside illustrations © Nick Abadzis 1999
Frightful Fouls
Text © Michael Coleman 1998, inside illustrations © Nick Abadzis 1998
Goal Greedy
Text © Michael Coleman 1998, inside illustations © Nick Abadzis 1998
The rights of Michael Coleman to be identified as the author
and of Nick Abadzis to be identified as the illustrator of this work
have been asserted by them in accordance with the
Copyright, Designs and Patents Act, 1988.
A CIP catalogue record for this book is available
from the British Library.
ISBN 978 1 84362 238 3
1 3 5 7 9 10 8 6 4 2 (hardback)
5 7 9 10 8 6 4 (paperback)
Printed in Great Britain
www.wattspublishing.co.uk

A HILARIOUS HAT TRICK OF STORIES!

 PAGE 7

 PAGE 69

 PAGE 131

ANGELS
f.c.

Goalkeeper

Left Full
Back

Right Full
Back

Midfield
(Centre)

Centre
Back

Striker

Coa

Kirsten
Browne

Barry 'Bazza'
Watts

Tarlock
Bhasin

Lennie
Gould
(Captain)

Daisy
Higgins

Colin 'Colly
Flower

DAZZLING

DRIBBLING

CONTENTS

1. Mike Sees a Problem!   10

2. Smash...or Grab!   26

3. Keep Your Eyes Peeled!   34

4. No Smoke Without Fire   44

5. A Red-Hot Display!   50

1

Mike Sees a Problem!

"How about these for next season, everybody?" said Trev brightly, dipping into the holdall at his feet. "I've been given them for nothing! What do you think?"

The Angels coach held the orange football shirt aloft. Seated in a semi-circle around him, the Angels players gaped silently up at it, then at each other, then back at the shirt again.

It was Lennie Gould, the Angels captain, who finally broke the silence. "Given 'em for nothing, do you say? Then you woz robbed, Trev!"

"Very witty, Lennie," laughed Trev. "Seriously, though. What do you really think of it?"

Mick Ryall, the team's tricky right midfield player, took off his glasses, blinked, put them back on again and said, "It's bright, Trev. It's definitely bright."

"Bright!" cried a shocked Bazza Watts. "It's near enough luminous, Mick! I've seen car headlamps that don't glow as much as that shirt!"

"Going to be playing night-time matches next season are we, Trev?" asked Lulu Squibb sarcastically. "Y'know, without any floodlights?"

11

"I thought you might like to try them out tomorrow," said Trev hesitantly, only to be met by groans from all corners of the room.

"Wear them tomorrow?" growled Lennie. "Against Hamley Hawks? Not likely! I mean – orange shirts! They'd think we were a right bunch of lemons!"

Trev frowned. In daily life the Angels

coach was the Reverend Trevor Rowe, vicar of St Jude's Church. All the Angels players were members of St Jude's Youth Club, and every year Trev led a shared weekend at the Leigh Country Park where they were joined by a group from another local youth club. This year it was to be the Hamley Hawks. The idea was that they all got to appreciate the countryside better by taking part in lots of different activities.

Everybody knew, though, that the highlight of the weekend was the Sunday afternoon football match between the two clubs. It was a game both teams were always desperate to win, because the tradition afterwards was for the losers to act as servants to the winners. In particular, this meant cleaning the huge dormitories that they used. Even though they only slept in them on the Saturday night, it was still a job which could take hours!

Sighing, Trev held up the orange shirt again. "Correct me if I'm wrong, but do I get the impression that none of you are very keen on this football shirt?"

"It *is* bright," nodded Mick Ryall, taking off his glasses again to peer at the shirt. "There's that to say for it."

"Spot on, Mick," said Colly Flower. "Trev, it's terrible. It's too bright. The only thing worse would be finding it came with orange shorts and orange socks as well."

"It *does* come with orange shorts and orange socks as well," said Trev, glumly pulling a pair of each from his holdall. "Not to mention…"

He dipped into the holdall one more time
and pulled out an altogether larger article,
"a matching top for the coach!"

Lennie led the Angels into a huddle.
Heads shook. Heads nodded. Finally, they
separated with a loud cheer.

Trev brightened. "That's a bit more like
it! Enthusiasm at last! You've made your
decision, have you?"

"We have, Trev. We'll stick to our old
white and blue strip – but you can keep
your orange top!"

Having settled the shirts question, Trev led the Angels out to the park's pitch for a six-a-side game before the Hamley group arrived. On the way he whispered in Mick's ear. "Nobody in the team can dribble like you, Mick. Nobody can send a defender the wrong way like you! So, once in a while I want you to go it alone. We'll call it Plan 7D. Seven, for your shirt number..."

"And D for 'Dribble'," said Mick. "Right?"

"It's D for 'Dazzling', actually," smiled Trev, "because that's what you'll need to be!"

It wasn't long before the coach decided to test his plan. Seeing Mick receive the ball on the right side of the pitch, Trev yelled, "Plan 7D, Mick!"

Mick looked up. Ahead of him were Ricky King, Rhoda O'Neill, Jeremy Emery and – in goal – Kirsten Browne. As Mick surged forward, Ricky came to meet him. Hardly slowing, Mick feinted to go to his left then, as Ricky moved that way, suddenly darted to the right and sprinted past him.

"Huh! You won't send *me* the wrong way," muttered Rhoda O'Neill, turning sideways on to force Mick to go outside her.

"Oh no?" cried Mick. Pretending to cut inside, then outside, then inside again, he caused Rhoda to spin like a top and finally lose her balance altogether as he went by.

Next in line was Jeremy Emery, the Angels tall and gangly defender. Determined not to be fooled into going the wrong way, he decided not to go any way at all. Planted with his feet wide apart, he stood solidly in Mick's path – only to find the ball quickly slipped through his legs!

"A nutmeg!" laughed Mick, scuttling past. There was only Kirsten to beat, now.

Taking careful aim for the bottom corner
of the net, he shaped to hit a screaming
shot – only to stop his foot a centimetre
from the ball. Like all the others, Kirsten
was sent completely the wrong way.
Soaring like an eagle towards one corner
of her goal she could only watch
helplessly as Mick calmly side-footed
the ball into the other corner!

"Plan 7D a total success!" cried Mick, running back for the kick-off.

"Make the most of it, Four-Eyes," growled a voice from nearby. "'Cos your dribbling won't send me the wrong way!"

Unnoticed, the Hamley Hawks group had arrived and were watching from the touchline. The boy who'd spoken was in the middle of them. He had a haircut like a mown lawn that hadn't had the edges trimmed. The others round him were nodding in agreement.

"Says who?" smiled Mick, taking off his glasses and wiping away a couple of spots of rain.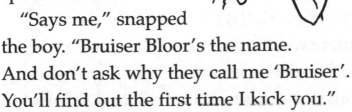

"Says me," snapped the boy. "Bruiser Bloor's the name. And don't ask why they call me 'Bruiser'. You'll find out the first time I kick you."

Laughing, the Hamley group went to huddle under a tree to stay dry. Mick shrugged and went back to the game. But, with the rain getting heavier, he found himself having to wipe his glasses more and more often. Finally he took them off altogether and held them in his hand.

"Plan 7D!" called Trev, as the ball was played out to Mick once more.

Mick looked up. In front of him Ricky King, Rhoda O'Neill, Jeremy Emery and Kirsten Browne were again barring his way.

Or were they? Without his glasses on, Mick really couldn't tell. Being very short-sighted, he could only see things really clearly if they were no more than a metre away. The trouble was, Ricky and the others *were* more than a metre away – which was why they all looked pretty blurry.

Undeterred, Mick zoomed off, dodging this way and that. Past Ricky King he went, then past Rhoda O'Neill – or so he thought until he heard Jonjo Rix shout, "What are you beating me for, Mick? I'm on your side!"

Squinting badly, Mick looked up. He wanted to be aiming for the goal, and that meant Kirsten, with Jeremy Emery somewhere in front of her. He couldn't see Kirsten, but...

Yes, not too far away he could definitely see tall, thin Jeremy! By the look of him, the defender had taken a handkerchief out to blow his nose. Very helpful!

Keeping his eyes fixed on the handkerchief, Mick raced forward. Drawing close, he shimmied one way, ducked the other, then raced past. "Sent you the wrong way again, Jez!" yelled Mick – only to be brought to a halt by the screech of Trev's whistle.

"Goal kick to us," called Kirsten from somewhere away to his left.

"What? How?"

"Put your glasses back on and you'll see," giggled Kirsten.

Mick did so – and groaned. The fuzzy defender he'd just waltzed round hadn't been a thin, nose-blowing Jeremy at all. It had been a corner flag!

Looking on, all but one of the Hamley Hawks players had collapsed with laughter. The exception was Bruiser Bloor. He merely smiled a nasty smile.

"Well, look at that," he said to the others. "We ain't going to need to rough up tricky Micky at all. Without his glasses, he's useless. All we've got to do is pinch 'em..."

He grinned his toothy grin as another thought came to him. "Either that, or bust 'em..."

2

Smash...or Grab!

By the time Mick Ryall and the other Angels
boys reached their dormitory after the
practice game, the Hamley Hawks boys
were already there. They'd taken over the
beds at one end of the dormitory – and had
already made a mess of it.

"Attention now!" called Trev. "Angels and
Hawks – I know it's tradition for the losing
team in the match on Sunday to clear up the
dormitory for the winners, but that doesn't
mean you shouldn't keep it tidy until then."

From behind his back Trev produced a stiff-bristled broom in one hand, and a brush and pan in the other. The broom he gave to Lennie Gould, the brush and pan to Bazza Watts. "Show them how it's done, lads. Start sweeping!"

As Lennie and Bazza started work, the others dumped their things on the beds. Mick Ryall went for the bed in the corner nearest the door. Taking off his glasses, he placed them carefully on the blanket while he removed his damp football shirt.

Immediately, Bruiser Bloor appeared at his elbow. After what Bloor had been like earlier, Mick was expecting more threats. But, no, the Hawks player seemed to be a changed person.

"Hi! I didn't mean what I said about kicking you, y'know. That was just my little joke. I wouldn't hurt a fly. Not even a flying Angel! Ha ha!"

Bloor laughed. And laughed...

"Ha-ha! Ha-ha-ha! Ha-ha-ha-ha!" he roared, holding his middle and tottering backwards and forwards until he was almost on top of Mick's bed...

"Ha-ha-ha-ha-yeeeeoooooowwwwww!!" Bloor spun round, holding his backside.

Behind him, holding the stiff-bristled broom that had just jabbed him like a hundred needles, stood Lennie Gould.

"Sorry and all that," Lennie apologised, "but you were just about to squash Mick's glasses. By accident, of course."

Bruiser Bloor gave a weak smile. "Was I? Phew! Good job you stopped me."

"I think I'd better put them back on," said Mick.

"Allow me," said Bloor. He plucked Mick's glasses from the bed - only to let them slip from his fingers. "Oops!"

"You've dropped them!" yelled Mick.

"Howzat!" shouted a voice.

They all looked down. Bazza Watts, sweeping under the bed, had thrust out his arm to give Mick's glasses a soft landing in a dustpan full of fluff!

"You sure your nickname's Bruiser?" growled Lennie. "Butterfingers Bloor would be nearer the mark."

"Phew!" breathed Bloor again. "You could be right. That was another close shave! I'd put those glasses somewhere safe if I was you, Mick."

"Yeah," Bazza said to Bloor. "Somewhere miles away from you."

Mick slipped them on. "There. That's where they're safest. And I won't take them off until bedtime!"

Poking his head through the top of his Arsenal pyjamas, Mick yawned. They'd had a busy afternoon and evening and he was worn out. Removing and folding his glasses, he placed them carefully in his bedside cabinet.

"Mick!" hissed Lennie. "You can't leave them in there!"

"Why not?" said Mick.

"Because Bloor could swipe them while you're asleep," whispered Bazza, scuttling across from his own bed. He was quickly joined by the other Angels players. "We reckon he could come after them, see? He knows that without your glasses you're...er..."

"Useless," said Mick, remembering his dribble round the corner flag.

"Can't you sleep with them on?" asked Jeremy Emery.

"No! That way, *I'd* bust them!"

"I know!" cried Lionel Murgatroyd. "How about staying awake and watching over them?"

"Good one, Lionel!" said Mick. "Then I'll fall asleep in the middle of the game tomorrow, so I'll still be useless!"

Lionel shook his head. "I didn't mean *you*, Mick. I meant *us*. We all take it in turns to guard your glasses for an hour."

"Brilliant!" said Lennie. "I'll do the first hour. Then I'll wake up Jonjo to do the second hour, he can wake up Tarlock for the third hour, and so on."

They all turned to Mick and helped tuck him into bed.

"Dazzling dreams, Mick," cooed Colly. "Your specs are as safe as anything. Your guardian Angels are here to look after them!"

❂   ❂   ❂

Sitting drowsily on the end of Mick's bed, Lionel glanced at his watch. By the pale light of the moon he saw that it said six minutes to four. Only another six minutes and he could wake up Ricky for his turn on guard duty.

Lionel's eyes began to droop. Quickly

he flicked them back open. He, of all people, couldn't go to sleep on duty! It had been his idea. A brilliant idea! They'd all said so.

He looked at his watch again. Five minutes to go. Maybe if he just stared at the watch face it would help him concentrate on staying awake.

Lionel focused hard. Four minutes to go. It was working! Three minutes to go. Two. One. Only sixty seconds to zero!

Zero, zero, zer…

zzzzzzzzzzzzzzz…

3

Keep Your Eyes Peeled!

Mick was dreaming. He was desperately
trying to set off on a mazy run through the
Hamley Hawks defence. The trouble was,
he couldn't move his feet. There seemed to
be a heavy weight on top of them...

Blinking open his eyes, Mick sat up in
bed – and discovered exactly why he'd been
having that particular dream. It was because
there *had* been a heavy weight on his feet.
A fast-asleep Lionel Murgatroyd!

"Lionel!" hissed Mick, giving him a shake.

"Wha-wha-wassamarra?" gurgled Lionel, suddenly sitting bolt upright. "Four o'clock, is it? Time I was off duty?"

Mick snorted. "Four o'clock? It's eight o'clock, Lionel! It's Sunday morning and we're at the Country Park and the sun's shining and all's right with the world and you've obviously been snoring when you should have been guarding...and...and..."

"And what?" said Lionel, still rubbing the sleep from his eyes.

"And," wailed Mick, staring at the wide open door of his bedside cabinet, "my glasses have gone!"

Waiting until the Hawks went off to breakfast, the Angels searched the dormitory from top to bottom. Finding nothing, they then confronted Bruiser Bloor, surrounding him as he finished off a huge plate of bacon and eggs.

"Admit it, Bloor," snarled Rhoda O'Neill, "you pinched Mick's glasses during the night, didn't you?"

"Me?" laughed Bloor. "I haven't even *seen* his glasses!" "A likely story," said Colly Flower. "It's true!" Bloor put on an injured look. "Hey, I know what you're up to. You're trying to frame me, aren't you?"

He turned to the other Hawks with a grin. "Get it? *Frame* me! Glasses, frames…"

A cry from Trev interrupted the stream of bad jokes.

"Attention everybody! I expect you're already thinking about this afternoon's match, but forget man-to-man marking and all that for now. This morning it's our Treasure Hunt. Sort yourselves into groups of four or five, then get instruction sheets from me. Visit all the destinations and solve all the clues to win a prize!"

"Trev really likes that orange top, doesn't he?" sighed Mick, looking across to where Trev was standing at the far end of the room. "He's still wearing it."

"That's it!" hissed Lionel Murgatroyd suddenly. "That's how we might find out who's got your glasses! Trev's just given us the answer!"

"By wearing orange?" asked Jonjo.

"No," replied Lionel, "by man-to-man marking! If our groups forget all about the Treasure Hunt and just follow the Hawks groups everywhere, maybe one of us will spot something..."

"Nothing," groaned Lionel. "We've been following them for miles and they haven't given us a clue."

Lionel, Kirsten, Jonjo, Rhoda and Colly,

together with a squinting Mick himself, had been trailing Bruiser Bloor's group, trying to keep themselves out of sight while they watched what the Hawks were doing. They'd just stopped as, through the trees, Bruiser Bloor had halted his group and looked their way.

Moments later the Hawks captain boomed, "I think we're being *goggled at*, team! So – let's go!"

Caught by surprise, the Angels group gave chase as the Hawks disappeared along a narrow track. But with Mick needing to go fairly slowly to avoid running into things, the Hawks were soon out of sight – and, by the time the Angels reached a signpost at a junction with a number of other tracks, they were nowhere to be seen.

Something else was, though. From the signpost a hastily scrawled note was fluttering.

"This is a 'dazzling dribbling' signpost," read Colly. "What sort of clue is that?"

"A bad joke Bruiser Bloor clue, if you ask me," said Lionel. He began to pace up and down. "Now, let's think. Mick's a dazzling dribbler…"

"Only when I'm wearing my glasses," said Mick glumly.

"Right. So a 'dazzling dribbling' signpost

could be…one with a pair of glasses! I bet Bloor's just got rid of the evidence by hiding them round here somewhere!"

They all dropped to their knees and scrabbled in the long grass at the base of the signpost. Suddenly, Lionel gave a cry of triumph. "Got them!" he cried, holding up Mick's glasses.

Mick couldn't have been happier if he'd just found a long-lost brother. Kissing his glasses, he rubbed them clean and put them on. But a worrying thought had struck Rhoda. She frowned.

"Why would Bloor leave a clue to help you find your glasses? That would be stupid."

Mick laughed as he gazed around. "Because Bloor *is* stupid! Now – which is the way back?"

They all looked up at the signpost. It clearly pointed them off along another, rather overgrown, track. With a spring in his step, Mick led the group down it. On they went, between trees and around brambles, as the track slowly got narrower and narrower...until finally it vanished altogether.

"Funny," said Kirsten. "That signpost definitely pointed this way."

Mick groaned. "Oh no! The note! I've just
realised what a 'dazzling dribbling' signpost
really is."

"What?" they all asked together.

"It's a signpost that sends you the wrong
way! Bloor must have switched it round.
That's why he didn't care about me finding
my glasses again – because his plan was for
us not to get back in time for the match.
And it worked. We're lost!"

4

No Smoke Without Fire

"Now what do we do?" asked Kirsten.

"Wait here," said Jonjo. "Trev and the other Angels will come looking for us when we don't turn up."

"But what if they meet Bruiser Bloor?" said Lionel. "And he sends them the wrong way too?"

"They'll never find us!" wailed Rhoda. "We'll miss the match! The Angels will only have half a team! They'll win! We'll have to be their slaves!"

"Bad," said Mick.

Rhoda looked panic-stricken. "Bad? It's terrible! You want to see the state of the girls' dormitory! We turned that over looking for your glasses, too!"

"Then we need to do something to show them where we are," said Mick. He took off his glasses and polished them thoughtfully. "But what?"

"Shout!" squawked Rhoda, and immediately began hollering at the top of her voice. "Help! We're here! Yoo-hooooo!!!"

The others joined in, calling at the tops of their voices, until Jonjo said, "It's no good. They won't hear us unless they're close. What we need is something to attract their attention from miles away."

Mick snapped his fingers. "I've got it! A smoke signal! They'd be able to see that from miles away!"

"Er...small problem, Mick," said Jonjo. "No smoke without fire. And no fire without matches."

"Wrong, Jonjo," said Mick, noticing the shafts of strong sunlight cutting through the trees. "You lot gather something to burn. I know how to light the fire!"

Soon they'd collected a pile of dry twigs and wet leaves. Taking them to a clearing so that there was no danger of the fire accidentally spreading, they heaped the sticks together. That was when Mick bent down...and took off his glasses once more.

Holding them up to the sky, he moved them around until the rays of the sun, shining through one of the lenses, came together in a sharp, hot point of light on the twigs. Within seconds the twigs started to smoulder. Not long after, they began to smoke. And then, with a sudden little *whoosh*, they burst into flame!

Whooping delightedly, the others helped tip more wood on top until they had a good, crackling fire. Then on went the wet leaves – and out billowed thick smoke!

"And now, Squaw Rhoda, send signals to Big Chief Trev the Rev!"

Grabbing her rucksack, Rhoda held it  over the bonfire so that some smoke became trapped underneath, then whipped it away to allow a big blob of smoke to sail upwards. Soon a flock of smoky dollops was sailing high into the sky, visible for miles around. And not long after that, there came the distant sounds of shouting and footsteps ploughing through the undergrowth.

Mick swung round. "Here comes Trev!"

Beside him, Lionel blinked. "Trev? Where?"

"You need your eyes tested, Lionel," said

Mick, pointing into the distance. "Can't you see his orange top?"

Lionel peered through the trees. "No."

Mick pointed again at the glow moving their way. "There!" He whipped his glasses off with a flourish. "Crikey, that top's so bright I can see it a mile away – and with only two eyes!" Slipping his glasses back on, Mick thumped his chest proudly. "We're saved, Lionel! Now brave Angels go fight afternoon battle with Hamley Hawks!" he cried. "And give them heap big whacking!"

5

A Red-Hot Display!

Bruiser Bloor moved menacingly to Mick's
side as the teams came out for the big
challenge match later that afternoon.

"You're going to wish you'd stayed lost in
the woods, Four-Eyes," he growled. "'Cos
I'm going to give you bruises so big you'll
be able to see 'em without your specs on!"

Bloor strode to his place in the Hamley
Hawks defence, while Mick trotted out to
his position on the right wing. Trev was
standing on the touchline with Lionel

Murgatroyd and Ricky King, the Angels substitutes.

"Remember the Angels code, Mick," said Trev, who'd overheard Bruiser's threat. "'Angels on and off the pitch.' No dirty play. The referee will sort him out if he gets near you."

"He isn't going to get near me, Trev!" laughed Mick, adjusting his glasses and gazing around the pitch. "Not now I can see him coming!"

And, as the game got underway, Mick proved to be as good as his word. He was in sparkling form.

When Bloor came thundering in to tackle him, Mick simply slipped the ball inside to Colly Flower or another Angels player, skipped over the Hawks player's flailing boots, then ran off to collect the return pass. After a few hopeless attempts, Bruiser stopped diving in and waited to see what Mick would do. When that happened Mick simply sent him the wrong way by dribbling up to him, feinting to go one way then darting the other before Bloor knew what had happened.

"Mick's playing brilliantly," said Trev to Lionel. "So…Plan 7D!" he hollered as the ball was pushed out to Mick yet again.

Hearing the call Mick set off at once, dribbling past one Hawks player after another. Approaching their penalty area, he was going at top speed.

Bruiser Bloor, finally realising what was happening, came racing in from the side and launched himself into a sliding tackle. But Mick had seen him coming. Stopping dead, his foot on the ball, he stood and watched as Bloor slithered in front of him like a snake in football gear. Only then did he set off again and clip the ball past the Hawks goalie and into the net.

1–0 to the Angels! Or was it?

Bruiser Bloor was still on the ground, holding his leg and yelling like mad. "Foul, ref! He trod on me! Send him off! I'm injured!"

"I didn't see anything," said the referee, puffing up.

"It was a foul, I tell you!" yelled Bloor. "He's broken my leg!"

With the referee starting to look more doubtful, Trev ran on to see what he could do to help. Behind him followed Lionel Murgatroyd holding the first-aid kit.

"I don't know what he's on about," hissed Mick to Lionel. "I didn't touch him!"

Trev bent down beside Bruiser. As he did so, the Hawks player let out an even louder cry of agony. "I'll never walk again! Just 'cos he wears glasses, it don't mean he's not dirty! Send him off, I say!"

"That's what he's on about!" said Lionel to Mick. "He's trying to get you sent off. He knows he can't cope with your dazzling dribbling…"

Even as he said the words, Lionel looked up into the sky – and had an idea.

Quickly taking Mick's glasses from him,
he hurried over to give Trev the first-aid
kit. Then, bending down beside him, he
held Mick's glasses up to the sun until
the hot dot of light was just where he
wanted it...

"Yeeeoooooooooowwwwwwwwww!!!"
screamed Bruiser Bloor. Moments later he'd
leapt to his feet, knocking Lionel flying as
he did so, and was racing round the penalty
area holding his backside.

"It seems like he can walk after all," said
the referee. "No foul! Goal allowed!"

"Looks like my glasses trick doesn't only set twigs on fire!" hooted Mick, hurrying across to Lionel. "Well done, Lionel!"

Lionel groaned. He seemed to be in pain.

"Are you all right?" said Mick. "You looked like you landed badly."

The Angels substitute lifted himself off the ground and pulled out something shapeless and mangled from beneath him.

He groaned again. "I did land badly. I landed on your glasses."

"That looks like the end of Plan 7D then, Mick," said Trev at half time. "Without your glasses you'll be beating players on our side as well as theirs."

Mick nodded glumly – until he suddenly realised that what Trev had said was wrong!

"No I won't, Trev," said Mick. "Because our players won't be trying to get the ball off me. The only players trying to tackle me will be Hawks, so I'll know they're the ones I have to beat!"

Feeling much happier, Mick scurried out for the start of the second half. He looked at the players around him. They were all very blurred and, unless he was quite close to them, even the Angels white shirts didn't look too much different to the blue shirts worn by the Hamley Hawks.

But that didn't matter. All he had to do was beat any player who came in to tackle him.

The chance came along fairly soon. Receiving a pass out on the touchline, Mick put his head down and raced towards the first blur.

"Come on then, Tricky Micky," growled the shape, "let's see you beat me."

It was Bruiser Bloor. Without slowing, Mick leaned to his left then dodged to his right. As he skipped past, though, the Hawks defender grabbed his arm and spun him round. Mick struggled free, the ball still at his feet. At once, Bloor seemed to give up. Mick's arm was released and he was away.

"No! Stop him!"

Hearing the shouts of alarm, Mick put a spurt on. Having escaped Bloor's clutches so easily, the Hawks obviously knew they were in trouble!

Side-stepping the first player who came towards him, he bamboozled the next and raced on. Now others were coming in to try to get the ball off him, desperate Hawks defenders complaining bitterly as he skipped round them.

Or were they Hawks defenders?

As he evaded another tackle, Mick thought he heard a voice, which sounded very much like that of Daisy Higgins, cry out, "I'm on your side!"

He dodged another tackle, this time to hear a voice sounding like Bazza Watts bellow, "Mick, you're going the wrong way!"

The wrong way? But how? Of course…

Bruiser Bloor! Spinning him round by the arm had been deliberate. That's why he hadn't given chase. He'd pointed him towards his own goal!

Mick screeched to a halt – but the damage had been done. Having taken the ball through his own defence, all the Hawks striker had to do was whip the ball off Mick's toe and whack it past Kirsten in the Angels goal to make the score 1–1!

Winning the ball back straight from the kick-off, Hamley Hawks swept forward, piling all their players into attack as they searched for the winner.

"Don't worry about him," yelled Bruiser Bloor to one of his defenders, who asked if he should stay back and mark Mick. "He won't be going anywhere."

To a miserable Lionel Murgatroyd, standing out on the touchline, it seemed as if Bloor was right. Mick was standing on his own on the halfway line, peering this way and that, as if he couldn't even work out which way to run if he did get the ball.

"It's all my fault," sighed Lionel. "It was me who busted his glasses."

"Don't blame yourself, Lionel," said Trev. "It's not your fault that Mick's short-sighted and can't see anything far off without glasses."

"He can see some things," replied Lionel. "Your orange shirt when you came looking for us, for instance. Mick didn't need his glasses on to see that."

"My orange—" began Trev.

He didn't finish. Instead, as a Hawks attack broke down and the ball was walloped upfield to relieve the pressure, he started sprinting.

"Plan 7D, Mick!" he yelled.

Out in the centre circle, Mick had the ball. With all the Hawks upfield he'd had the time he'd needed to bring it under control. He looked up. As ever, the grass and pitch markings nearby were in clear focus but everything looked blurry in the distance.

Even so, he could make out something. An orange blur, now coming to a halt somewhere far off.

And then he heard Trev's call. "Aim for the orange shirt!"

Mick set off, the ball at his feet, his eyes fixed on the orange target. On he ran until, suddenly, a goalkeeper-shaped blur emerged. A duck and a dodge and Mick was past him, still running, running, until another shape appeared – that of the Hawks goal and, standing right behind the net, Trev in his bright orange top!

All Mick had to do was run the ball between the posts!

2–1 to Angels!

From there on, Hamley Hawks couldn't leave Mick alone, and all the Angels had to do was play out time to win the match. As Bruiser Bloor and his team-mates skulked off to start cleaning the dormitories, the players crowded round to congratulate Mick.

"Thank Trev," said Mick. "I could see his

orange top miles away!"

Lennie Gould stepped forward. "Then on behalf of the team, Trev, I'd like to say thank you very much for wearing that top…" Then, grinning at the others, he added, "…although it's still the most revolting colour in the world and none of us would be seen dead in it!"

"I suppose you're right," said Trev. "OK, forget the orange shirts. We stick to *angelic* white!"

"You've got to keep wearing that top though, Trev," said Mick amid the cheering.

"Why?" chorused the Angels.

"In case I smash my glasses again, of course. As far as I'm concerned that top of Trev's is a sight for sore eyes!"

FRIGHTFUL FOULS

CONTENTS

1. Slow off the Mark   72

2. Run, Daisy, Run!   87

3. Seeing Double   97

4. Popping up Everywhere!   103

5. Tackling the Problem   114

Slow off the Mark

"Byron!" yelled Daisy Higgins. "If you don't shift yourself, I'm going to be late for the kick-off!"

The lanky figure lying on the sofa looked up, then rolled over and made itself comfortable again.

Daisy glared. Having an elder brother was bad enough, but having a bone-idle, sofa-snoozing elder brother was even worse – especially when he'd promised to come along to the Angels match and take some photographs of her in action.

"Wake up!" she yelled. "Emergency! Fire! Earthquake! Byron, the ceiling's about to collapse!"

"Right," yawned Byron. "Call me when it's all over."

Daisy took another look at the clock. Should she just go? No, she decided grimly. Byron had known about this match for weeks. The lazy article was going to move.

Picking up her brother's heavy camera bag off the floor, she hoisted it high in the air. Then, deciding she wasn't holding it quite high enough, she stood on a chair.

"Byron," cooed Daisy. "Roll on to your back, Bruv. You'll be more comfy."

"Good thinking," murmured Byron. Eyes still closed, he turned over. That was when Daisy let the camera bag fall.

As the heavy bag landed on Byron's stomach he let out a cry of pain and shot bolt upright.

"What did you do that for?" he moaned.

"I was only trying to help," said Daisy sweetly. "I didn't want you to forget your camera. You'll need it to take pictures, won't you?"

Byron rolled off the sofa with a sigh. Unzipping one of the camera bag's pockets, he began fishing inside.

"OK, OK. Let me check my films first. Am I going to need a fast film or a slow one?"

"What's the difference?" said Daisy.

"If I'm going to be taking pictures of fast-moving things I'll need a fast film, otherwise the pictures will come out blurred. If I'm going to photograph something slow-moving then a slow film will be good enough."

"What sort of film do you think you need?" exclaimed Daisy. "You're going to be taking action shots of me!"

"Right. Got you," nodded Byron. "A slow film it is then."

Angels' opponents were Beeston Stingers, a team who competed in a different league competition to them. The two teams had been invited to play in a two-legged match for the Inter-League Challenge Trophy.

"I hear their front runner's good," said Jeremy Emery as he and Daisy trotted out on to the pitch. "Really fast."

"Fast?" said a lean and wiry boy coming alongside them. "He's faster than fast. More like greased lightning! That's why they called him 'Zippy'. Zippy Larkin. Number ten, he is."

Daisy sniffed, pretending not to care. "Greased lightning, eh? That all?"

"Yeah," said the boy. "Take a good look. 'Cos this is about the last time you'll get near me!" Then, poking his tongue out, he suddenly sprinted away from them, the number ten on his shirt dancing wildly as he ran.

"Number 10," said Jeremy. "That's him. Zippy Larkin. Wow! Look at him go! You could have a problem today, Daisy."

Daisy scowled. "Not as big a problem as he's going to have if he pokes his tongue out at me again!"

For a while, Daisy didn't see Zippy Larkin – but this was because the Angels began the match in sparkling form. With Lennie Gould, the team captain, and Rhoda O'Neill winning lots of tackles in midfield, the Angels were well on top but unable to score. Then, after about twenty minutes of play, Beeston Stingers broke away.

A quick pass reached Zippy Larkin, who brought the ball smoothly under control. Greased lightning, eh? thought Daisy. She decided not to dive into the tackle, but keep her distance. If he wanted to get past her from where he was, Zippy-Dippy was going to have to give her five metres start. And nobody was *that* fast.

She was wrong. Zippy *was* that fast. As he prodded the ball past her, Daisy turned and started running as quickly as she could.

Snapetty-snapetty-snap!

The whirring of Byron's camera from his spot on the touchline told Daisy that the scene had been caught on film... unfortunately. For within just a few strides Zippy Larkin, his tongue poking out and his legs pumping like pistons, was flashing past her. All she could do was puff behind him and applaud when Kirsten Browne in the Angels goal pulled off a wonderful save from Zippy's shot.

"Where did you get to?" sniggered the Beeston player as he trotted back. "You're going to have to move a bit faster than that!"

Oh, yes? thought Daisy. There was more than one way of undoing a Zippy! If he could run that fast then she'd just prevent him getting started! With her new tactic in mind, Daisy didn't hang back as another quick ball was played out of the Beeston defence. Sailing in, she slid along the ground to whip the ball off Zippy Larkin's toe.

At least, that had been the plan. But even as Daisy slid through, out poked Zippy's tongue and he was off with the ball at his feet. This time, not even Kirsten could stop him. On he ran to slam the ball past her. Beeston were 1–0 up!

And so it went on. For the rest of the first half, and on into the second, Daisy felt like she was trying to tackle a greyhound wearing football boots. Only good covering by Tarlock Bhasin and Jeremy Emery kept Zippy Larkin at bay.

With twenty minutes left and Angels still 0–1 behind, Daisy decided that enough was enough. She'd tried standing off. She'd tried sliding in. There was only one thing she hadn't tried. And so, as Zippy Larkin went to race past her yet again, she tried it. Not even bothering to run, Daisy simply put her hands on her hips and stepped into his path.

Snappety-snappety-snap!

Byron's camera captured the scene
perfectly. Zippy Larkin bounced off
Daisy as though he'd hit a trampoline at
top speed.

"*Frightful* foul, Number Four," shouted
the referee, racing over. "Yellow card! Do it
again and you'll be sent off!"

Daisy's match was over anyway. Shaking his head solemnly, Trevor Rowe, the Angels coach, immediately called her off and sent on substitute Ricky King in her place.

"Daisy, I'm ashamed of you," said Trev. "Remember the Angels code: 'Angels on and off the pitch'. That was a deliberate foul."

"It wasn't deliberate," pleaded Daisy. "He's so fast I was simply trying to make him go the long way round!

Trev didn't seem impressed. Out on the pitch, the much speedier Ricky King was keeping Zippy Larkin quiet.

As the final whistle blew, with Beeston Stingers still 1–0 ahead, Daisy trudged silently away. She had a problem all right – and, before the second-leg match, she had to solve it.

⚽   ⚽   ⚽

"If I don't do something," she grumbled next day, "Trev's going to leave me out of the second-leg game and play Ricky instead."

From behind the door of the small cupboard Byron used as a dark-room for developing his photographs came a shout of joy. "Yes!"

"It's nothing to be pleased about!" yelled Daisy.

The door creaked open and Byron's face appeared. "I wasn't pleased about that. I was pleased about these!"

Reaching into the cupboard he pulled
out the two photographs he'd taken of her
during the game: one showing her running
flat out, but with Zippy Larkin streaking
ahead of her – and the other of her standing,
hands on hips, as he was about to bounce
into her! That would have been bad enough.
But, worst of all, Byron had produced
life-sized versions!

"First time I've tried it," he said cheerfully. "Came out well, didn't they? I know Zippy's a bit of a blur, but you're nice and clear."

"Get rid of them!" yelled Daisy. "I don't want to be nice and clear! I want to be nice and fast!"

Byron shrugged. Tossing the pictures back into the cupboard he stretched himself out on the sofa as Daisy began pacing up and down.

"I've got to get faster somehow," she said, thinking aloud. "Training, that's what I need. A week's solid speed training…"

"Speed training, eh?" said a voice from the depths of the sofa. Byron popped his head up. "Now I can help you with that as well, y'know…"

2

Run, Daisy, Run!

Daisy looked at her brother in astonishment.

"You?" she said. "*You* could help me run faster? You can't even get yourself off that sofa!"

Byron levered himself up on to his elbows. He looked strangely awake, as if he'd just had an enthusiasm injection.

"Ah," he said, "but why do I lie on the sofa? Have you asked yourself that?"

"Because you're lazy," said Daisy.

"Wrong," said Byron. "One of the reasons

I've been lying here lately is to recover from my afternoon bursts of speed training – namely, my paper round."

"Your paper round? That's not speed training!"

"Of course it is. When I first started, it took me an hour. Last Friday it only took me thirty minutes. If that's not speeding up, I don't know what is."

Daisy had no answer. Byron had started his paper round a fortnight ago. For most of that time he'd gone out at four o'clock in the afternoon and come back at five. But last Friday he'd certainly got home much earlier. Perhaps her brother was right...

"So," said Daisy uncertainly, "what's your thinking?"

"Simple," replied Byron. "You can do my round all next week. I'll tell the papershop owner I'm ill and that you're going to do it for me. Come Saturday you'll be faster, as well. Zippy Larkin won't know what's hit him!"

Was there a flaw in the plan somewhere? If there was, Daisy couldn't see it. Any activity that had improved Byron's speed could only work wonders on her. "OK," she said, "I'll do it!"

✸   ✸   ✸

"Aren't you coming with me?" asked Daisy just before four o'clock the following afternoon.

Byron shook his head. "I'd love to, but I've already rung the shop to say I've hurt my leg and that you're doing my round for me. Besides, somebody's got to time you, haven't they?"

With a flourish, he pulled a stop-watch out from beneath the sofa cushion his head was resting on. "On your marks! Get set! Go!"

Daisy raced down the path and leapt on to her bike. Pedalling furiously across town she collected the newspapers. From there it was just a short ride to where they had to be delivered – to thirty or so flats in a huge, ten-storey tower block.

Locking her bike, Daisy dashed to the first flat on the round: number 101. Pushing a newspaper through the letterbox she sprinted down to the next, then to the next. By the time she'd done all her deliveries on the ground floor she was puffing and panting, but happy. A week of this, thought Daisy, and a quick sprint on a football pitch would seem nothing. Zippy Larkin, watch out!

She checked the newspapers in her bag. Next stop, the fourth floor. Daisy raced along to the lift – only to groan as she saw the sign taped to its doors:

She was going to have to run up the stairs! Taking a deep breath, she set off. Up to the fourth floor she went, then to the sixth, then to the seventh – until finally she had just one newspaper left to deliver. Daisy looked at the number scrawled on its front: number 1001. On the tenth floor!

By the time she reached it, she was exhausted. Slamming the newspaper through number 1001's letterbox, Daisy sank to her knees. She'd done it!

Panting for breath, she didn't realise the door behind her had clicked open. Then she heard a familiar voice.

"Well, well. If it isn't Daisy the Dawdler."

Daisy turned. It was Zippy Larkin, a newspaper in his hand. His flat was the last on Byron's list. Daisy tried to struggle to her feet.

"We'll see who's the dawdler on Saturday," she gasped.

"I reckon I'm going to see it sooner than that," sneered Zippy. "I reckon I'm going to see it right now." He held out the newspaper Daisy had just shoved through his letterbox. "This is 101's paper, see? You must have stuck our one in their door. So go on – dawdle off and fetch it!"

By the time she'd gone down to the bottom and crawled back up again, Daisy was whacked out.

"I've seen snails moving faster than you!" hooted Zippy.

Stung by the Beeston player's taunts, Daisy lost her temper. "That's because I'm injured," she lied. "I was injured on Saturday, too. But I'll be fine by the end of the week – and then you'll see. I'll outrun you any day!"

"Any day?" said Zippy Larkin at once. "Right. Make it Thursday."

"What?"

"Six o'clock, our training ground. I do some sprinting practice before the others turn up for the training session. I'll race you then."

Daisy gulped. "Six o'clock? Thursday?"

"You got it. Be there if you dare!"

3

Seeing Double

Daisy crawled indoors – to come face to face
with herself in the hallway! The photograph
Byron had taken of her with her hands on her
hips had been turned into a life-sized cardboard
cut-out and was propped up against the end wall.

Byron called out from the sofa in the lounge.
"What do you reckon then?"

Daisy stomped in to join him – only to find a
second cut-out leaning against the lounge wall.
Byron had made it from the picture of Daisy
going at full steam.

"Good, eh?" laughed Byron. "Without Zippy Larkin bombing away from you, you look like you're going really fast!" He looked at his watch. "Which just goes to show that the camera can lie. Where have you been? Talk about slow! You've taken ages!"

"I had to walk up all the stairs," moaned Daisy. "The lift wasn't working!"

"What, again?" Byron shook his head. "It wasn't working last week, either. Not until Friday…"

Friday? Suddenly, Daisy understood. She'd been tricked! Thundering across the room, she launched herself onto her brother.

"You toad! You lazy, good-for-nothing toad!" she yelled, sitting on him so that he couldn't move. "You speeded up doing your paper round last Friday, all right. But not because *you* were faster. Because the lift was working!"

"Gerroff!" squawked Byron.

But Daisy was in no mood to get off. "Because of you, I've challenged Zippy Larkin to a race!" She bounced on Byron for good measure. "And when I turn up and get beaten by a mile..." Bounce! "...that's going to give him so much confidence..." Bounce! "...I'll have as much chance of catching him on Saturday as a tortoise with a bad leg!" Bounce! Bounce! Bounce!

"Aagh!" groaned Byron. "Gerroff! Mum's home!"

Hearing the sound of the key in the front door, Daisy reluctantly began to move. Things were bad enough as it was without her getting into trouble for turning her brother into a pancake.

Even before she'd got to her feet, though, she heard her mum's voice coming from the hallway.

"Daisy! What on earth are you doing in your football gear at this time of the day?"

Daisy looked down at her jeans and
T-shirt. In her football gear? What was
her mum on about? And what was she
saying now?

"You know, if you dressed in something
other than an Angels FC shirt I don't think I'd
recognise you!"

Suddenly, Daisy realised what must be
happening. She peeped out into the hallway
just as her mum sighed, "Oh, don't just stand
there. Come and help me get the tea ready!"
then marched off to the kitchen.

She'd been talking to the Daisy cut-out! It was so life-like, her own mum had been fooled into thinking it was really her!

But if it was that life-like, then… maybe…

"Byron!" she squeaked, rushing back into the lounge and grabbing the other cut-out, the one showing her running flat out. "I can beat Zippy Larkin. I know I can!"

"How? Ride a bike?"

"Yes, exactly! Except it won't be me riding it. It'll be somebody else, with this cut-out tied to them so that he thinks it's really me!"

"Somebody else? Who's gonna agree to do a daft thing like that?"

"You are, Bruv," snarled Daisy, "or I'm going to pick up the phone and…"

4

Popping Up Everywhere!

In the end, Byron hadn't taken a lot of persuading. By threatening to tell the papershop owner that he hadn't had a bad leg at all, Daisy had made her brother see sense.

"You sure this is going to work?" muttered Byron.

"It will if you're as quick at riding your bike as you are at diving on to the sofa," said Daisy.

They were in the lane which ran alongside the Beeston Stingers ground. It was a perfect spot to carry out Daisy's plan. A waist-high fence ran the length of the lane. Every few metres, tall clumps of the thick bushes which skirted the Beeston ground hid the view.

Daisy moved to a bush-free spot and looked across towards the Stingers' changing rooms. Zippy Larkin was just coming out, carrying a traffic cone in each hand.

"Here he comes, Bruv. Get ready."

Hidden behind the thickest clump of bushes, Byron unwrapped two copies of the running Daisy cut-out. Then, as he sat astride his bike, Daisy tied them on either side of him. She squinted at her brother. Perfect! Crouched down, and with his bike hidden by the fence, Zippy wouldn't be able to see Byron at all!

Daisy peered through a small gap in the fence. Zippy Larkin had placed one of the cones almost opposite where she was.

She watched as he trotted to put the other
cone down about forty metres further along.
Perfect again! He was planning to sprint to a
spot opposite another thick clump of bushes
further down the lane.

It was as he was jogging back to the start
that Daisy popped up, moved along to a
clear spot between the bushes, and called
out to him.

"That's it, is it? Your sprinting practice?"

Zippy gave her a withering look. "This is just jogging. Get over here if you want that race. Then you'll see some real running."

"I'm fine here," called Daisy. "The lane's flat enough for me."

Zippy snorted. "Please yourself. You've got no chance wherever you are." He pointed. "Down as far as that cone, right?"

It was Daisy's turn to snort. "Is that all?

What's that, halfway for wimps? Make it
there and back."

"There and back?" Zippy Larkin hooted.
"You won't even be there by the time I'm
back!"

"We'll see," called Daisy. "Go on, get to
your marks. You can say 'Go'."

As Zippy strolled across to the start cone, Daisy ducked as if she was crouching to begin the race.

"Get ready, Byron!" she hissed. "As soon as he says 'Go!', start pedalling! And make it good, Bruv!"

On his side of the fence Zippy Larkin crouched. He glanced across. There was no sign of Daisy. He assumed she must be doing the same on her side of the fence. She'd pop up again when he said "Go!" – and that's the last he would see of her until the race was over!

"On your marks," he called. "Get set! Go!"

Zippy launched himself forward. Out of the corner of his eye he saw a shape wearing an Angels football shirt do the same. Tongue out now, he began to race across the grass towards the far cone. Glancing casually to one side, he fully expected to be ahead. But he wasn't!

She was still with him, flashing between the gaps in the bushes! In fact – she was moving ahead!

Still crouched on her side of the fence, Daisy watched Byron pedalling hard towards the end of the lane. This was going to be the tricky bit. Could he turn without mishap? Yes, he could! In a blur of dust, she saw Byron skid round in a half-circle and, almost without slowing down, begin racing back towards her.

Zippy Larkin rounded the far cone unable to believe his own eyes. Daisy Higgins was going like the wind. What's more, she was getting further and further ahead of him!

He put in a final spurt, but it was no good. She'd disappeared behind the clump of bushes opposite the finish long before he reached it.

Peering through the tiniest of openings, Daisy saw a look of suspicion cross Zippy Larkin's face.

"Get out of sight, Byron!" she hissed.

Zippy was already hurrying across to the fence. But, by the time he got there, Byron had already shot round the corner. The only person he saw was Daisy, as she stood up and ambled casually towards him.

"Ah, there you are at last," said Daisy. "You weren't too zippy, Zippy!"

The Beeston player leaned over the fence and looked up and down the lane. Seeing nothing, his face fell.

"You…you…" he spluttered.

"Can run fast?" trilled Daisy. "You'd better believe it!"

From the look on Zippy's face it was obvious that he'd been completely fooled. And not only him. Further across the pitch the rest of the Beeston squad had arrived for their training session and had seen the end of the race. Even from where she was, Daisy could hear their shocked voices.

"Zippy – she beat Zippy!"

"Crikey! There's no point him trying to outrun her on Saturday!"

Daisy winked. "I reckon I agree with them, Zip. Don't you?" she said.

"No!" cried Zippy. He took another forlorn look up and down the lane. "I'll race you again. Come on, right now!"

Daisy shook her head and laughed. "Sorry, Zip. You'll have to wait until the match on Saturday. You can race me then – if you dare!"

5

Tackling the Problem

"A little reminder, just before the kick-off," said Daisy on Saturday morning. "That should do the trick."

Byron looked at her suspiciously. "How do you mean, a little reminder?"

"Don't worry, Bruv. You just get yourself, those cut-outs and your bike into that lane, and be ready to belt along it like you did before. I'll be over to tell you when."

Arriving at the Beeston ground early, Daisy got changed quickly and raced out onto the

pitch before anybody else. She hared
right over to the fence where, as far as
anybody could see, she was practising
her ball-juggling.

"Are you there, Byron?" she hissed at the
bush nearest the start of the lane.

"Yes, I'm here," came the answer. "Get a
move on, Daisy."

Daisy looked over towards the changing
rooms. Others were coming out now, Zippy
Larkin amongst them. Seeing some of the
Beeston players nudge him and point her
way, she deliberately lobbed the ball into the
lane and hopped over the fence after it.

"Go, Byron!" she hissed, ducking down out of sight beneath the fence.

Once again Byron shot off along the lane just as he'd done before, making it look as if Daisy was chasing after the ball at blinding speed. Skid-turning at the end of the lane, he raced back to the cover of the bushes.

"Is that it now?" he gasped as Daisy stood up again, tossed the ball back over the fence, then hopped over after it.

On the far side of the pitch, she could see all the Beeston players standing in a line, their mouths open. In the middle of them, Zippy Larkin was shaking his head in utter amazement.

"Yep, you can leave it there, Byron!" said Daisy out of the side of her mouth. "Little old Zippy looks like he's seen a ghost. He won't be trying to outrun me today!"

And, for the whole of the first half, Daisy was right.

Every time the ball came to Zippy Larkin, he would look anxiously in her direction and immediately pass the ball to somebody else. Not once did he turn and try to outrun her.

It made all the difference. With Zippy quiet, the Angels defence weren't under too much pressure. Jeremy Emery, released from having to cover for Daisy, was able to venture forward into midfield. Winning the ball with a strong tackle he sent Rhoda O'Neill away. She played a quick wall pass with Mick Ryall, collected the return, and without hesitation drilled a low shot into the Beeston net.

1–0 to Angels! Now the teams were level at 1–1 on aggregate!

As the half went on, Zippy's confidence sank even lower. His passes started going astray. Then, anxiously looking behind him for Daisy, he tripped over the ball. Daisy, trundling forward at her own speed, was able to collect the ball and slide it out to Jonjo Rix. Racing down to the byline, the Angels forward whipped over a cross pass for Rhoda O'Neill to belt into the Beeston net.

2–0 to Angels! Now they were 2–1 ahead on aggregate!

"Keep this up and we'll be fine," said Trev at half-time. He turned to Daisy. "I don't know what you've done to Zippy Larkin, Daisy, but you've got him in your pocket!"

Byron was standing further along the touchline. Trotting past him as she ran back on to the pitch, Daisy gave him a thumbs-up sign.

"Working a treat, isn't it?" she crowed. "Not poking his tongue out at me today, is he?"

It was true, too. Throughout the whole of the first half, Zippy Larkin's tongue had stayed firmly out of sight.

What's more, with the unhappy Beeston striker still not daring to try to outrun Daisy, out of sight was where it stayed. As the match entered its final ten minutes, Daisy was beginning to think she'd never had an easier game.

Increasingly desperate now, Beeston Stingers launched another attack. But once again, as the ball was played forward to him, the uncertain Zippy Larkin failed to bring it under control properly. Moving in, Daisy decided to waste a bit of time. Taking careful aim, she walloped the ball first bounce over the fence and into the lane.

"Go get it, Zippy!" yelled somebody. "There's not long left!"

The Beeston striker immediately raced off, his tongue poking out, to clamber over the fence. Watching him go, Daisy took the opportunity of another quick chat with Byron on the touchline.

"That must be the fastest old Zip's run today," she giggled.

But her brother wasn't listening. In fact, Byron was giving every impression of not wanting to hang around at all. Smiling nervously, he began to edge away.

"Right. Yeah. Well – got to go now, Daisy. Things to do…"

Daisy frowned. Then, as she saw Zippy Larkin toss the ball over the fence but then stop as if he'd spotted something else, her frown changed to a look of horror.

"Byron! The cut-outs! You didn't leave them…"

But her brother was already on the move. "It's all your fault. 'You can leave it there, Byron' – that's what you said! So I did! Both of them!"

"And he's found them!" groaned Daisy.

Zippy Larkin had climbed back over the fence, the Daisy cut-outs under his arm.

Moments later he'd dumped them on the
ground, jumped up and down on them,
and was sprinting like the wind back to
the pitch.

"Right," he snarled at Daisy. "By the time
I've finished with you, you're gonna feel
like you *are* a cardboard cut-out." He swung
round to his team-mates and screamed.
"Stingers! Gimme the ball!"

His team-mates did just that. From the
throw-in, the ball landed straight at Zippy's
feet. Daisy didn't know what to do. Should

she tackle him or not? Unable to decide, she
ventured forward slightly. Zippy reacted
immediately. Pushing the ball past her he
paused just long enough to poke out his
tongue before racing off.

Enraged, Daisy turned and gave chase.
In front of her, Zippy was angling in
towards the Angels penalty box. She'd
never catch him! Suddenly he slowed
down as the ball caught a bump and
bobbled into the air. Now she could!

Flying forward, Daisy stretched out a leg and stabbed at the ball with the end of her toe – only to watch it fly up into the air, over Kirsten's head and into the Angels net!

2–1 to Angels, but now 2–2 on aggregate!

"Same again in a minute," snapped the furious Zippy, racing back for the kick-off.

Daisy gulped. She didn't doubt it. He was going to get the ball and run at her again, and poke his tongue out at her again and...

Poke his tongue out?

Suddenly it came to her. She'd seen it in the photographs too, she'd thought it was a nasty trick he did whenever he outran an opponent. But – he'd done the same thing when he raced over to get the ball from the lane. He hadn't been racing past anybody then...just racing.

It must be a habit, Daisy realised, something Zippy couldn't help doing! Poke tongue, start sprinting! So maybe if she was to watch his mouth and not the ball…

The Angels kicked off. But, inspired by the goal and Zippy Larkin's sudden return to form, Beeston quickly won the ball back.

"Gimme, gimme, gimme!" screamed Zippy Larkin.

Daisy moved towards him. As the ball came towards him Zippy brought it under control and turned, his eyes gleaming – and his mouth shut. Daisy moved in closer…closer…

Suddenly she saw his lips begin to part and his tongue appear. It had to be the sign. He was about to sprint past her. She had to tackle him now!

Wallop!

Daisy timed her tackle perfectly. Leaping forward, she blocked the ball just as Zippy Larkin began to sprint. Propelled by his own speed, the Stingers player shot forward and flew through the air like a cannonball.

"Foul!" he screamed.

"Play on!" shouted the referee. "Perfectly good tackle!"

This wasn't what the Beeston defence had been expecting. Standing still, they were completely wrong-footed as Daisy moved forward and lobbed the ball over their heads.

All Jonjo Rix had to do was run on to her pass, sweep round their goalie and plant the ball into the Stingers net.

3–1 to Angels. 3–2 on aggregate!

Five minutes later, with Zippy Larkin still moaning that he'd been fouled, the final whistle blew. Trev immediately raced over to congratulate Daisy.

"Well done, Daisy! That was a tricky opponent you had to deal with. He hasn't got that nickname for nothing, you know."

"Too right, Trev!" said Daisy. "He's pretty fast is, er…what's his nickname again?"

"Zippy!"

Daisy clicked her fingers. "Zippy. Of course." She laughed. "It was on the tip of my tongue!"

GOAL

GREEDY

CONTENTS

1. Superior Skill   134

2. Tarlock goes for Goal   148

3. I Want to be Alone!   158

4. Nought out of Ten!   167

5. Goal Shy!   176

1

Superior Skill

"Don't think about football all the time!"

Trevor Rowe – the vicar of St Jude's Church and Angels FC's coach – had given his team this advice after the last training session. "Come along to Youth Club on Friday evening and forget about the game for a while," he'd said.

And come along they had. Walking through the club-room door, Trev gave a satisfied nod. The players had obviously taken his advice. Club Night was in full swing with, as far as Trev could see, the whole squad enjoying a relaxing break from football.

Or were they?

What was the exciting and noisy game that Kirsten Browne, Mick Ryall, Lennie Gould and Lulu Squibb were playing in one corner of the club room? Trev looked more closely and saw that they were playing…bar football!

Beyond them, Ricky King, Jonjo Rix, Lionel Murgatroyd and Bazza Watts were bent over the pool table.

At least they've taken my advice, thought Trev – until he saw that they were only using the smooth baize surface as an ideal pitch for the club's table football set!

With a sigh, Trev wandered over to where Daisy Higgins, Rhoda O'Neill, Jeremy Emery and Colly Flower were playing cards. Surely *they* were taking time away from football? But, as he got closer, the Angels coach heard Daisy say, "You mean to say not one of you knows who won the F.A. Cup in 1963? West Ham United, of course." They were using football quiz cards!

Didn't any of his squad ever take a break from football? Twelve of them clearly didn't. Tarlock Bhasin was his only hope. The Angels defender was sitting in an armchair, quietly reading. Trev strolled across to him.

"Hello, Tarlock. What are you reading?"

Tarlock looked up. "Hi, Trev. It's a classic."

Trev beamed. "A classic, eh? Good lad. What is it? *Treasure Island? Oliver Twist?*"

"Not likely," said Tarlock. He lifted the cover for Trev to see. *"The Illustrated History of Manchester United,"* said Tarlock. "You want to read it, Trev. It's a real classic!"

Knowing when he was beaten, Trev laughed. Football fanatics, that's what they were! Still, at least it meant that his next job should be easy.

"OK, listen everybody!" he called out.

Around the room the bar footballers stopped clunking, the table soccer players stopped flicking and the football quizzers stopped quizzing. Tarlock even put his book down...

Until, that is, Trev added, "I'm looking for a volunteer to do a job."

At once, the clunking, flicking and quizzing started up again. Only Tarlock didn't go back to what he'd been doing. He asked, "A volunteer to do what, Trev?"

"Funny you should ask, Tarlock," said Trev, raising his voice so that he could be heard by everybody. "A volunteer to do a job...connected with football.

The reaction couldn't have been more immediate if the Angels coach had said he'd got five-pound notes to give away. Clunking, flicking and quizzing were instantly abandoned in the sudden rush to Trev's side.

"What sort of job, Trev?" said Lennie Gould, the team's skipper. "Ballboy for a Wembley International?"

"Full-time mascot to the England team?" said Lionel Murgatroyd.

"Full-time mascot to the England *women's* team?" asked Lulu Squibb, giving Lionel a jab in the ribs while she was at it.

A flurry of equally fabulous suggestions came from the other players as they gathered eagerly round.

"I see I've got your full attention at last," laughed Trev. "So I'll finish what I was saying. I'm looking for a volunteer to do a job connected with football... *writing*."

"Writing?" said Bazza Watts, as the Angels players frowned at each other. "Like...with a pen and paper?"

"Words and sentences and stuff?" asked Mick Ryall.

Jeremy Emery sucked his teeth doubtfully. "And spelling?"

Trev nodded. "Well done, team. You've got it in one. So, who's interested in doing some football writing?"

There was a short silence. Then…

…*clunk* went a bar football. *Flick* went a table soccer player. *Shuffle* went a deck of football quiz cards. Within a minute, everybody had drifted back to what they'd been doing. Except Tarlock.

"Football writing?" he asked. "How do you mean, Trev?"

"I mean," said Trev, "writing a report of our match against Totton Tykes for the junior section of this week's *Sporting Pink*."

"The *Sporting Pink*?" gasped Tarlock. "The Saturday evening football paper?"

"You read it?" asked Trev.

"When I can get hold of it," said Tarlock. "My father reads it from cover to cover! And then he starts from the front again!"

"Well, this week he could be reading *your* report, Tarlock! I've just heard that Angels FC are to be Saturday's featured team. If there's enough room, they'll print a report from us."

"Wow!"

"So I thought," said Trev, pretending not to notice as the clunks, flicks and quiz questions

faded again, "that it would be a nice idea if
one of the players wrote it rather than me.
And as you seem to be the only volunteer,
Tarlock…the job's yours!"

"Wow!" said Tarlock again.

Trev gazed around the now silent club
room. Open-mouthed, everybody was
staring Tarlock's way.

"Happy writing," Trev said to him.
"And by the look of it, the *Sporting Pink* is
going to sell at least thirteen extra copies
this week!"

✦ ✦ ✦

"Hello, son," said Mr Bhasin as Tarlock
arrived home. "Did you have a good time?"

"Great!" said Tarlock. "You'll never guess
what Trev wants me to do..."

Glancing at his father, Tarlock saw the
Sporting Pink nestling on his lap. He must
have been reading it through for the second
or third time, as usual.

How delighted he'll be, thought
Tarlock, to read a report in that very
newspaper, written by his own son!

Especially, he thought suddenly, if his son's name is mentioned. Maybe in the headline even! Possibilities began to pop into Tarlock's mind...

'Brilliant Bhasin!'

'Terrific Tarlock!'

His daydream was interrupted by Mr Bhasin asking, "So? What does Trev want you to do?"

Tarlock was on the point of telling his father all about the match report when he stopped himself.

Why not keep it a secret? What a surprise it would be for his father when he opened the paper next Saturday! Oh, the look on his face would be wonderful!

So, instead, Tarlock said, "He wants me to...play for the Angels on Saturday."

"Oh," said Mr Bhasin, frowning. "Good. Very good, son."

Sitting on his bed, a cheerful Tarlock doodled a few more headlines on a sheet of paper.

Suddenly, a nasty thought occurred to him. What if he didn't play well? What if he had one of those games when nothing went right? He could hardly put his own name in the match report then, could he?

The more he thought about it, the more Tarlock realised that he was going to have to do something during the game that would justify giving himself a mention in his report. But what?

The answer came in a flash. *Score a goal, that's what!* Goalscorers were always named, even if they'd been completely awful for the rest of the game. What's more, goalscorers regularly hit the headlines, too.

'*Bang 'em in Bhasin!*'

'*Ten-goal Tarlock Trounces Totton Tykes!*'

Yes, that was it. All he had to do was score a goal on Saturday and his name would be there for his father to read.

A perfect solution! Well, fairly perfect. There was, realised Tarlock, just one slight problem. He would actually have to *score* a goal.

And not once, in all the games he'd played for Angels FC, had he ever come close to doing that...

2

Tarlock goes for Goal

So it was a determined Tarlock who stepped onto the pitch for the regular Angels training session on Tuesday evening.

Practice, he'd decided, that's all he needed. If he could get into the habit of banging in goals during training, then he wouldn't be able to stop himself scoring in the real match!

"Two laps of the pitch to warm up," shouted Trev as usual.

Tarlock began to jog steadily – only to find the others whistling past him from all sides.

"Come on, Tarlock!" shouted Daisy Higgins as she shot by. "The sooner we finish Trev's exercises, the sooner we can get on with the practice match!"

And so it went on, with the dribbling-round-cones exercise more like racing-round-cones and their press-ups more like hurry-ups as everybody tried to get them finished as quickly as possible.

But why? Tarlock couldn't figure it out. And it got no clearer when Trev finally got them into the practice match, half an hour earlier than usual…

Straight from the kick-off, Rhoda O'Neill won the ball and began to dribble towards the goal. When this happened, Tarlock the defender would normally stay put on the halfway line. Not today, though! Eager to get his goal-scoring habits on the move, Tarlock launched himself forward to join the attack. Charging into a clear space in the penalty area, he screamed for a pass.

"Rhoda!!"

But the pass didn't come. Ignoring him completely, Rhoda tried a shot which went whistling into the net.

Three minutes later, exactly the same thing happened again. Tarlock was up with the attack as Mick Ryall raced into the penalty area.

"Mick!!"

But, once again, the pass didn't come as Mick Ryall ignored him and ran on to whack the ball into the net himself.

Trudging back to the centre spot, Tarlock thought hard. The signs weren't good. Obviously, the others weren't used to him joining the attacks. But if they weren't going to spot his runs and pass to him, what could he do? The answer came as he won the ball in the centre of the field. Not pass to *them*, of course!

He set off on a mazy dribble. Past one player, then another, then another. This was the way to do it! In front of him he only had Kirsten Browne, the Angels goalie, to beat. As she came out to meet him, Tarlock dummied to go one way, then took the ball the other.

All he had to do was tap the ball into the empty net… And he would have done just that, if Colly Flower hadn't raced in and done it for him!

"I was going to score that!" yelled Tarlock.

Colly shrugged. "Sorry, Tarlock. I couldn't stop myself. Must be my natural striker's instinct, I reckon. Hey, you could mention that in your report, y'know…"

In his report? So that was it! That's why the whole team had been so goal greedy that evening.

He'd realised that the one sure-fire way of getting his name in the paper was to score a goal – and so had *they*! He was trying to practise goal-scoring – and so were they! And they were better at it than he was!

If the ball was even going to be whipped off his toe as he dribbled through, how could he score?

By not dribbling, Tarlock told himself as he picked up the ball some thirty metres out from goal. By firing in a shot from long distance!

Taking a few steps forward, he looked up. There was a clear gap to aim at. Gritting his teeth, Tarlock lined up to thump in a beauty of a shot. Leaving his foot like a missile, the ball hurtled, barely a metre off the ground, towards the goal. It had to go in...

"Goal!! Yeahh!!" shouted Jonjo Rix.

Tarlock couldn't believe his eyes. Just as his rocket shot had been destined for the left-hand corner of the net, the Angels striker had thrown himself forward and diverted it with a diving header into the other corner!

⚽   ⚽   ⚽

"What about that for a cracker?" said Jonjo to Tarlock when they got back into the changing room. "Do one of those on

Saturday and you'll have to mention me!"

"And me," chipped in Colly. "Striker's instinct, remember."

"And me," said Rhoda O'Neill and Mick Ryall together.

Tarlock slumped disconsolately onto a bench. With this sort of competition he stood no chance of scoring. He was just going to have to find another reason for putting his own name in the article. But what?

He gazed around, looking for inspiration. The scene might have inspired an article about rubbish tips, but that was about it. The changing room was a total mess. There were bags, boots and items of kit everywhere as the Angels players changed back from being footballers to their everyday selves.

Their everyday selves...that was it!

Next to him, Jonjo was still talking about his goal. "A headline header, that's what I'd call it. What d'you reckon, Tarlock?"

"I don't know," said Tarlock. "I was thinking of a different sort of article."

"Different?" said Jonjo. All around the changing room, eyes swung their way. "How do you mean, different?"

"More of a behind-the-scenes article. One that mentions interesting things the players do off the pitch. Hobbies, that sort of thing."

Even as he said it, ideas were popping into his head…

TOUCHLINES AND HEADLINES
When Tarlock Bhasin, the star Angels FC defender, isn't playing football he enjoys nothing better than writing articles about it.

He smiled at the others.

"Interesting facts about the players," he said. "Yes, I think that's what this article's going to need."

3

I Want to be Alone!

Tarlock hurried home from school the next day. He wanted to get cracking on his article, but...Wednesday was Jobs Day. Before his parents got home he had to empty the rubbish bins and tidy his room. They'd also been given a stack of Maths and English homework. Until that lot was done, article-writing was out of the question.

He'd just started on his room when the doorbell rang. It was Daisy Higgins and she was holding a basketball under her arm.

"Hello, Tarlock. I'm not bothering you, am I? Only I thought you'd like to know something really interesting."

Before Tarlock could answer, Daisy flipped the basketball up into the air, spun it hard, and balanced it on the tip of her finger. "Basketball spinning," she said, proudly. "My record is seven minutes, eleven seconds. That's an interesting bit for your article, isn't it?"

"Not as interesting as this!" came a shout.

Scooting up the drive on a swish skateboard was Jeremy Emery. As he reached them he spun round, flipped the skateboard into the air, then jumped on it again to set off back down the drive.

"What do you think, Tarlock?" he called over his shoulder. "You could say something like, 'When Jeremy isn't performing sliding tackles, he enjoys sliding in a different way!'"

"Funny you should mention sliding," said another voice. "Because that's what my hobby is about – sort of."

Lionel Murgatroyd had arrived. Over his shoulder he was carrying a canvas bag that looked as if it weighed a ton.

Staggering past Daisy, he let down his load and flipped open the bag.

Tarlock blinked. "Marbles?"

"You've got it, Tarlock!" said Lionel, brightly. "Two thousand, one hundred and twenty four of them. Tortoiseshell, Cat's Eyes, Red Devils, Speckled Spanglers…you name it, I've got one. Now admit it – you can't get anything much more interesting than that, can you?"

"Oh, yes you can!"

It was Bazza Watts, carrying a small box with round holes in the side. "Forget basketballs, skateboards and marbles, Tarlock. My furry pet here is the most interesting thing you'll see all year."

"A furry pet?" laughed Daisy, still basketball-spinning. "What is it? The world's most interesting hamster?"

"Or gerbil?" said Jeremy, skateboarding past.

"Or rabbit?" asked Lionel, getting close.

"Tarantula spider, actually," said Bazza, whipping the top off the box.

The effect was electric. Discovering that his nose was just inches from the furriest and largest spider he'd ever seen in his life, Lionel leapt in the air.

"Waa!!" he screamed – and knocked over his marbles sack at the same time.

"Wee!!" cried Daisy as she suddenly found two thousand marbles rolling beneath her feet – and let her spinning basketball spin away.

"Woo!!" yelled Jeremy Emery as he executed a perfect double back-flip – only to land on a runaway basketball, swerve wildly out of control, and knock over the dustbin which Tarlock had just finished filling.

"Don't worry, we'll help you clear up the mess," yelled a chorus from the front gate.

It was Lennie Gould, along with the remainder of the Angels squad, each of them clutching toys, pets, photograph albums, collections of football programmes and goodness knew what else. Lennie winked. "And after that we'll all show you our interesting hobbies, Tarlock!"

"We can't wait to see our names in the paper, y'know," said Daisy, once the garden had been tidied and the dustbin refilled.

Tarlock sighed. He was wishing he'd never had the idea of a behind-the-scenes article. Not only had he now got far too much information, none of his jobs had been finished either.

"I don't reckon anybody's name is going to be in the paper," he said, "because I don't think I'm going to have time to write anything. I've got too many jobs to do here first."

"You've got to!" cried Lulu Squibb. "I've told everybody to look out for it."

"Me too," said Colly Flower. "We all have."

It was Bazza Watts who accidentally gave Tarlock his next idea. "What other jobs have you got to do, then?" he asked.

"We'll all help you. Won't we, guys?" The whole Angels squad nodded in agreement.

Help? Why not, thought Tarlock. It would be a fair swap – their names in his article in return for being able to put his feet up for a couple of days.

"We-ll…" said Tarlock slowly. "There's my room to tidy. And my homework to do…"

"Leave it all to us," said Bazza at once. "Lulu, Daisy and Lionel – you three do the Maths. Except for Lennie, the rest of you can sort out Tarlock's room."

"What about you, then?" asked Rhoda O'Neill. "What are you two going to do?"

"Me and Lennie will do the English," said Bazza. "'Cos English is *deferably* our *bestest* subject of all, ain't it!"

4

Nought out of Ten!

Tarlock felt more than pleased with himself the next morning. Not only had he been praised for having a tidier room than ever, he was certain there'd soon be some good homework marks coming his way too.

"All done?" said Tarlock as he met the others.

"All done," said Daisy, handing over the Maths.

"And here's your English essay," said Lennie Gould, giving Tarlock some sheets of paper. "No problem."

"Once we'd worked out what your title was," said Bazza Watts. "I hope you make your writing a bit neater for your match report, Tarlock. I don't want to pick up the paper and see that a great goal was scored by somebody called Wazza Batts!"

"Or Loony Gold," laughed Lennie.

Tarlock handed the work in straight away. It was Parents' Evening that night and he fully expected to get some glowing praise when his father came back from talking to his teachers...

He was half right. When Mr Bhasin came back that evening he was certainly glowing – but not with praise.

"Tarlock! This is terrible!" exclaimed Mr Bhasin, waving some sheets of paper. "Explain yourself!"

Taking the pages from his father, Tarlock saw that it was the essay Bazza and

Lennie had written for him. And, in bright red on the front page, was the mark:

Nought out of ten!

Beneath it, was his teacher's note: "You were supposed to write an essay entitled 'My Favourite Book' – not an essay about fishing, entitled 'My Favourite Hook'!"

Tarlock groaned. Bazza had said they'd had trouble reading the title. They'd written him an essay on the wrong subject!

"Father, I can explain," he said.

"I hope so. Your work has never received such a bad mark before."

"That's just it," said Tarlock, cheerfully. "It *isn't* my work. Somebody did it for me!"

"Somebody did it for you?"

"That's right. And they made a big mistake. They thought…" Tarlock didn't get a chance to finish. If Mr Bhasin looked angry before, that was nothing to the way he looked now.

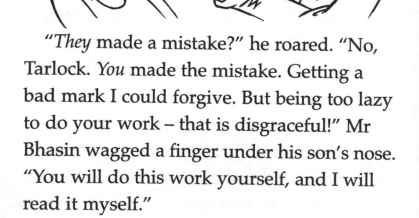

"*They* made a mistake?" he roared. "No, Tarlock. *You* made the mistake. Getting a bad mark I could forgive. But being too lazy to do your work – that is disgraceful!" Mr Bhasin wagged a finger under his son's nose. "You will do this work yourself, and I will read it myself."

"Yes, father," said Tarlock glumly.

"You will do it on Saturday."

"Yes, father. I'll do it straight after playing football."

"No, Tarlock. You will do it *instead* of playing football. I will take you to the library at nine-thirty and I will pick you up again at twelve-thirty. You will spend the three hours in between forgetting all about football and writing a perfect essay."

⚽   ⚽   ⚽

Tarlock sat miserably in his room. He'd always known that doing something to get his name in the match report wasn't going to be easy. But without actually playing in the match it was going to be impossible!

But playing, banging in a goal, writing his report, delivering it to the newspaper offices, writing his English essay *and* being at the library when his father arrived to pick him up was impossible too!

Or was it? Totton Tykes played their games in the park across the road from the library. And the newspaper offices weren't far away from there, either. Tarlock drew up a possible plan...

09.30 Dropped at library by father.

09.35 Leave library and go across road to park.

10.00 Kick off, play match, score brilliant goal, finish match.

11.15 Leave park, go back to library.

11:20 Write match report mentioning brilliant goal.

12:15 Deliver report to newspaper office.

12:30 Be waiting on library steps when father arrives.

Easy!

Of course, he had to write his English essay too. Tarlock did that on Friday night, hiding under the bedcovers.

Next morning, bleary-eyed but with a finished essay in his bag, he put on his Angels FC shirt, shorts and socks under his normal clothes. Then, tying his boots round his neck, he tucked them under his jacket.

"I will be back for you at twelve-thirty, remember," called Mr Bhasin as he drove away from the library steps. Tarlock waited until he saw the car turn the corner, then he sprinted across the road, through the park gates, and into the changing room.

"Here comes the ace reporter," cried Jonjo Rix.

"Hope you've got a stack of pencils, Tarlock," said Mick Ryall. "I reckon you're going to have a lot of writing to do."

Lennie Gould clapped Tarlock on the shoulder. "Talk about raring to go," he said, waving at the excited Angels players. "Poor old Totton will know they've been in a game today!"

Know they've been in a game today...

As Lennie's words sank in, Tarlock's heart fell like a lead weight. How could he mention himself in the report?

If he did that, his father would know
he'd played in the match after being
forbidden to.

No, he couldn't mention himself. But if he
scored a goal, he'd have to mention himself.
Which meant…

Tarlock groaned. It meant that, much as
he'd love to, he simply mustn't score!

"No goal today either, then," he sighed.
"Oh, well. What's new?"

5

Goal Shy!

Tarlock had never seen his team so fired
up. Racing out from the changing room,
they almost left scorch marks on the grass
in their eagerness to get to the pitch. Just as
well he was no longer trying to score a
goal, thought Tarlock. From the look of the
other Angels, he'd be lucky to get a touch
of the ball!

And for the first fifty minutes of the
sixty-minute match he was right. The
Angels ran riot.

No sooner had Totton Tykes kicked off than Rhoda O'Neill won the ball with a lightning tackle. Playing a one-two with Jonjo Rix, she raced through and cracked home a scorcher from the edge of the penalty area.

1–0 to Angels after just twenty seconds!

From then on, goals flew in at regular intervals as the team went mad. All Tarlock had to do was stand on the halfway line and try to commit to memory what was going on in front of him...

1 min. *Rhoda O'Neill – cracking shot from edge of area. 1–0.*

4 mins. *Jonjo Rix –
dribbled round goalie. 2–0.*

12 mins. *Colly Flower – bullet header.
3–0.*

21 mins. *Mick Ryall – mazy run
and shot. 4–0.*

24 mins. *Jeremy Emery – header from corner kick. 5–0.*

28 mins. *Bazza Watts –*
hopeful thump from
long way out. 6–0.

Half time.

31 mins. *Lulu Squibb –*
backward diving header. 7–0.

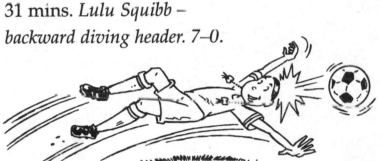

34 mins. *Lennie Gould – beat six players (one of*
them twice) before rounding the goalkeeper. 8–0.

37 mins. *Daisy Higgins –*
header from corner, after
shoving Jeremy Emery
aside with a shout of,
"Oi, it's my turn!".
9–0.

39 mins. *Ricky King –*
raced through to score just
twenty seconds after coming
on as substitute. 10–0.

46 mins. *Lionel Murgatroyd – came on as*
second substitute and scored with a
complete miskick which sent
the Tykes' goalie the
wrong way.
11–0.

50 mins. Kirsten Browne –
penalty kick. 12–0.

Yes, even Kirsten, the Angels goalkeeper,
had got herself on the score-sheet! That
would make twelve names to go in the
report. The interesting facts will have to go,
thought Tarlock. He turned, ready to stroll
back for yet another kick-off.

"Tarlock!" It was Lennie Gould, calling to
him as he ran over. "You're the only one
who hasn't scored!"

"I know. I'm not worried."

"But we are!" said Lennie. The whole Angels team was looking his way. "Come on – you've got ten minutes to do it in."

"No, it doesn't matter…"

"Of course it does," said Colly Flower, nudging Tarlock forward. "Go on, Tarlock. I'll stand around and do nothing in your position. You can play striker for the rest of the game."

Slowly, Tarlock trotted upfield to the striker's position alongside Jonjo Rix. Lennie had said he had ten minutes. He had meant ten minutes to score a goal. Little did he guess that if a chance came Tarlock's way he was going to have to miss it on purpose!

And a chance did come, almost immediately. Sweeping past a miserable Totton defender, Rhoda O'Neill played a delightful ball through.

"Go, Tarlock!" she yelled.

Tarlock ran on to it, the dispirited Totton players not even bothering to give chase. Getting the ball under control, he looked up. The Totton goalkeeper was coming off his line, leaving himself open for a chip over his head.

Leaning back, Tarlock shaped up to do just that – only to deliberately hit the ball much too hard and send it whizzing miles over the bar.

"Bad luck, Tarlock!" yelled Lennie. "It'll come!"

A couple of minutes drifted by. Then, out on the left, Ricky King began a flying run down the wing.

"Into the middle, Tarlock!" yelled Lulu Squibb.

Reaching the byline, Ricky pulled back a perfect pass. Tarlock brought the ball under control, took careful aim – and thumped a powerful shot which, far from going into the net, almost uprooted the corner flag!

And so it went on. Put through yet again, Tarlock deliberately kicked the ground first so that the ball trickled like a slow-motion snail up to the surprised Totton goalie. Then, as Mick Ryall squared an inch-perfect cross for him, he pretended to slip over while the ball skidded away to safety.

"Not my day," he said to Lennie Gould with a shrug. "Thanks anyway."

"Tarlock," said a determined Lennie. "It is going to be your day. All you've got to do is stick with me...now!"

Launching himself into a tackle, the Angels captain emerged with the ball and set off on a winding dribble. Past one Totton player after another he went. As he trotted dutifully behind, Tarlock had a nasty feeling he knew what Lennie was planning to do.

He was right. Dribbling on into the area,
Lennie waited for the Totton goalie to come
out to meet him. Moments later the keeper
was sitting in the mud, not bothering to get
up as Lennie dribbled past him.

"Tarlock!" yelled Lennie. "Come on, tap
it in!"

Thinking he was making Tarlock's day,
the Angels captain had stopped the ball
right on the goal-line. All he had to do was
nudge it over the line to score!

There was no way out. With the ball just sitting on the line he could hardly kick it wide. And he definitely couldn't get it over the bar! Tarlock trudged miserably towards the ball, about to become the unhappiest goalscorer in the history of the game…

As Tarlock heard the referee's whistle blow he was still a stride away from the ball. It was full-time! The end of the game! Angels FC had won 12–0 and he *hadn't* scored!

Tarlock didn't know whether to laugh or cry.

The moment the letter-box rattled, Mr Bhasin leapt to his feet. When he returned, a cheerful look on his face, he settled back in his chair with the *Sporting Pink* across his knees.

From his spot in front of the television, Tarlock couldn't help giving a sigh of relief. His plan had worked out. After the match he'd dashed back to the library, written his match report mentioning everybody's name except his own, then shot down to the newspaper offices to deliver it.

At least the rest of the Angels would be happy, even if he wasn't. And perhaps he'd have a chance to write another report one day...

"Tarlock," said Mr Bhasin, looking up from the paper.

"Yes, Father?"

"Did you play football today?"

"Me? How could I? You said I wasn't allowed."

"Then perhaps you can explain this," growled Mr Bhasin, menacingly.

Tarlock took the newspaper from him, confident that he could explain his way out of anything. He hadn't scored, after all. In the long report he'd written, his was the only name that hadn't been mentioned.

"Oh, no!" he groaned.

Too late, he remembered what Trev had said when he first told him about the Angels being the featured team. *If there's enough room, they'll print a report from us.*

As Tarlock looked at the pink page, it was obvious that there hadn't been enough room for his long report. But there had been sufficient room for a rewritten version taking up just a couple of lines:

Bhasin Draws A Blank!

Angels FC swept to a crushing victory by 12–0 against Totton Tykes, with every player in the squad scoring except for defender Tarlock Bhasin!